THE USBORNE
FIRST BOOK OF NUMBERS

Angela Wilkes and Claudia Zeff
Illustrated by Stephen Cartwright
Consultant: Wyn Brooks

CONTENTS

This little duck is hiding on each double page. Can you find him?

How many?

0 zero

1 one

2 two

3 three

4 four

5 five

6 six

7 seven

8 eight

9 nine

10 ten

11 eleven

12 twelve

13 thirteen

14 fourteen

15 fifteen

16 sixteen

17 seventeen

18 eighteen

19 nineteen

20 twenty

4

Number Patterns

Are they the same?

Count the bricks piled up on top of each other.

Are there the same number of bricks here?

Count the children standing in a line.

Are there the same number of children playing?

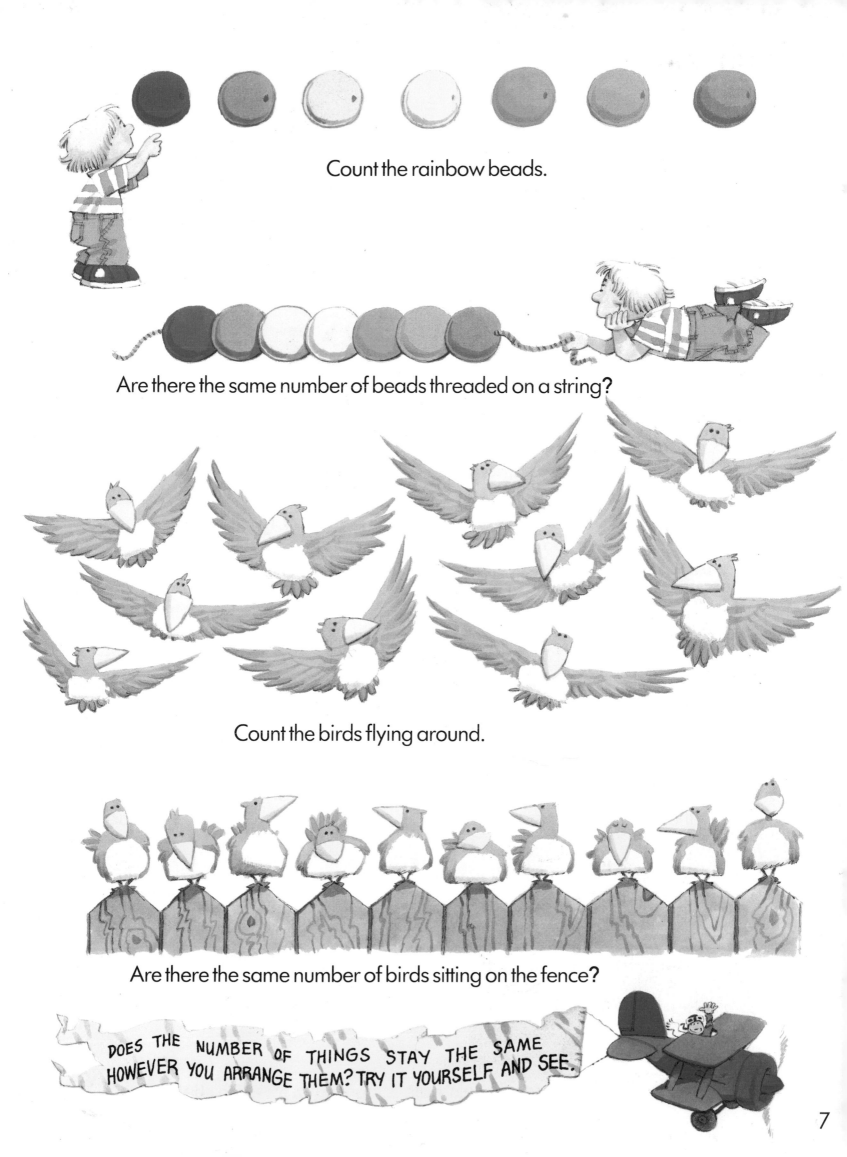

Count the rainbow beads.

Are there the same number of beads threaded on a string?

Count the birds flying around.

Are there the same number of birds sitting on the fence?

DOES THE NUMBER OF THINGS STAY THE SAME HOWEVER YOU ARRANGE THEM? TRY IT YOURSELF AND SEE.

Sets

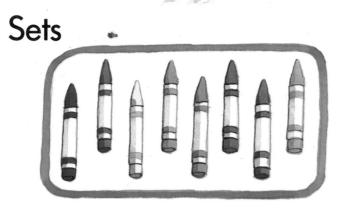

Here is a set of 8 crayons. To show a set we draw a boundary around the things.

We say the toys are members of the set. How many are there? The cars are a subset.

How many members are there in each set? Which set has 7 members in it? Which set has the most members in it? Which has the fewest?

This set of people can be partitioned. How many are there in each of the subsets?

The geese and pigs are subsets of the set of farm animals. How many in each subset?

Match the set of chefs to the set of chefs' hats. Is there a hat for each chef?

Is there a bonnet for each baby? Is there a rattle for each baby? Match them and see.

This is Clever Clogs. He is very good at counting. He knows that 2 is less than 3 and 4 is greater than 3. He can write this in a special code using two signs he knows. < means less than and > means greater than.
So Clever Clogs can write 2<3 and 4>3. Can you read the code?
Has he put the right signs between the sets below? Count them and see.

Satpal the snake charmer has 3 cobras in his basket. They come out when he plays his pipe.

His friend Rafat is also a snake charmer, but his cobras have escaped. His basket is empty.

Here are the sets of snakes. Satpal has 3 and Rafat has 0. When a set has no members it is called an empty set.

One hundred crows

How many crows are there in each row?
How many crows are there in each column?
How many crows are wearing pink goggles?
Can you find 12 crows wearing top hats?
Are there more crows with pink goggles or with top hats?
Are there more crows with scarves or with cases?

Can you find 7 crows wearing flying helmets?
How many crows are looking for worms?
How many crows have managed to find them?
Can you see any other sets of crows?
How many sets of 10 crows are there?
Are any two sets the same?
How many crows are there altogether?

This is what 1,000 crows look like. The picture was made by printing 100 crows ten times. (They had to make them smaller to fit on the page). Can you imagine what 1 million (1,000,000) crows would look like?

Comparing things

How many apples are there on this tree? Are there more red apples than gold apples?

Has this tree more red apples or fewer red apples than the first tree?

Christmas time

Ben Sally Tim

I HAVE MORE PRESENTS THAN YOU!

BUT I HAVE EVEN MORE THAN YOU!

Who has the most presents? What about Ben?

The Three Witches

Beth Peg Doris

Which nasty witch has the most things in her evil brew? Who has the most spiders?

Who has the most frogs and who has the fewest? Who has more frogs than cats?

Which is the odd one out in each of these groups?

Matching Clothes

Can you find a coat for everyone?
Are there enough gloves for each child
to have a pair?

Can you find boots for everyone?
Will all the children have a scarf and hat?
Do you think it is summer or winter?

In the right order

10th
tenth

9th
ninth

8th
eighth

7th
seventh

6th
sixth

5th
fifth

4th
fourth

3rd
third

2nd
second

1st
first

Who is on the first step of the ladder?
What is on the fifth step?
Who do you think will be next to reach the top step?

The race

The red runner is in first place. Who is coming last?

Who has won the race? Who has come second?

The hold-up

How many outlaws are on top of the first carriage? What is happening on top of the second carriage?

Which carriage has the most people inside it? What do you think will happen next in the hold-up?

Which cat comes next?

The cats in the top row are in sequence. Which cat from the bottom row should be next in line in the top row?

It is a busy time at the Grand Hotel. Look closely at the picture and you will see all kinds of strange things happening.
What is happening on the first floor?
On which floors are people having baths?
Who has let go of the balloon?

Where in the hotel do people have tea?
Who is having trouble finding something?
If you got out of the lift on the fourth floor and walked into the first room, what would you see? What do you think is happening?
Where are the burglars?

15

Adding up

Here are two sets of rabbits. There are 4 rabbits in one set and 3 in the other.

If you put the two sets together, it makes 7 rabbits. Count them and check.

+ is the symbol for 'putting together' or adding.
= is the symbol for 'is the same as' or 'is equal to'.
Clever Clogs can write about the rabbits in his code.
4 and 3 together make 7 is $4 + 3 = 7$

Puppy count

$4 + 2 = 6$. Can you put this into words? Count the puppies and check the answer.

These three bricklayers are building a wall. They have already laid 3 bricks and they are carrying 3 more.

How many bricks have the builders laid altogether?

These tightrope walkers are wearing safety ropes to hold them on the number line. How many are there altogether? How many more would you need to make 10?

The adding square

Clever Clogs has made a magic square that can add up any two numbers under 10. Here are the instructions he gives to his friends to explain how it works.
"Run one finger down from a green number and one finger along from a pink number and the answer will be the black number where your fingers meet".
Try it out. What is 3 + 5? How many other ways can you make 8 on the square? Do the 8's make a pattern? How many ways can you make 11 on the square?

+	0	1	2	3	4	5	6	7	8	9	10
0	0	1	2	3	4	5	6	7	8	9	10
1	1	2	3	4	5	6	7	8	9	10	11
2	2	3	4	5	6	7	8	9	10	11	12
3	3	4	5	6	7	8	9	10	11	12	13
4	4	5	6	7	8	9	10	11	12	13	14
5	5	6	7	8	9	10	11	12	13	14	15
6	6	7	8	9	10	11	12	13	14	15	16
7	7	8	9	10	11	12	13	14	15	16	17
8	8	9	10	11	12	13	14	15	16	17	18
9	9	10	11	12	13	14	15	16	17	18	19
10	10	11	12	13	14	15	16	17	18	19	20

The story of 12 maze

Jo is lost in a maze and his friend Simon is trying to find him. The only way he can find him is by jumping over the signs that add up to 12. You can use the magic square to help Simon find Jo. Follow the route with your finger.

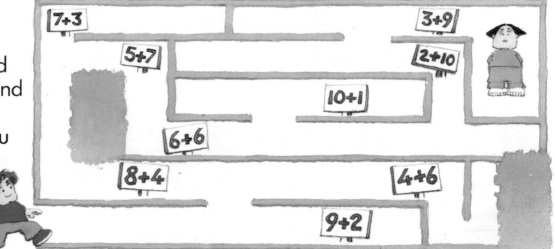

Taking away

There are 8 lovely green apples on a plate until Clever Clogs eats 3 of them.

Now there are 5 apples left on the plate. Clever Clogs can write this in code as $8 - 3 = 5$.

This bear has 5 pots of honey on his shelf.

He eats 3 for breakfast. How many are left?

Count the moles

You can count backwards to take away. Put your finger on 8 and hop to each number until you reach 5. How many hops? How many moles went to look for worms?

Detective Gotcha

These 6 robbers are creeping away from a museum with their sacks full of precious things.

The amazing Detective Gotcha sees their footprints and catches 2 of them. How many got away? Is the code 2 + 4 = 6 or 6 − 2 = 4?

Circus muddle

If the clowns left the ring, how many performers would be left?

If the clowns and the jugglers left, how many would be left?

Which is the smallest set, the clowns, the jugglers or the acrobats?

Which set has the most members?

How many performers are there altogether?

The long  and short of it

The stork is taller than the baby and the duck is shorter than both of them. Who is the tallest? Who is the shortest?

The gorilla is fatter than the lady and the man is thinner than both of them. Who is the fattest? Who is the thinnest?

Which is the highest?
Which is the lowest?

The dinosaur is longer than the snake. The snake is longer than the worm. Who is the longest? Look at the curled-up worm. Do you think it is longer or shorter than the straight worm?

The Jones family

Who is the tallest in the family?
Who is shorter, Daniel or Emily?
Is there anything smaller than Daniel?

Who is the smallest grown-up in the family?
Who is the fattest grown-up in the family?
What is the smallest thing in the picture?

Measuring with parts of your body

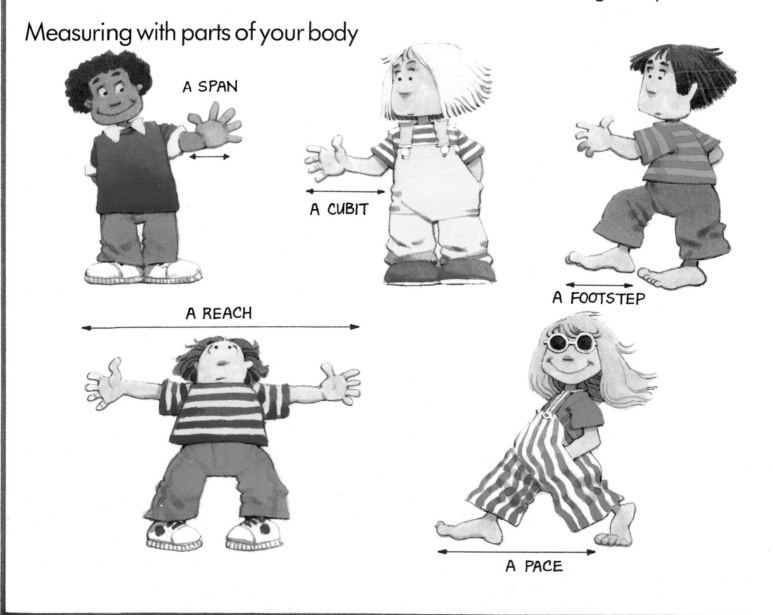

A SPAN

A CUBIT

A FOOTSTEP

A REACH

A PACE

Heavy weights and light weights

Heavy things

Light things

Balancing

Which is heavier, the lion or the mouse?
How can you tell just by looking?

Is this cat heavier than the pile of sand?
How much do you think the cat weighs?

Now there is enough sand to balance the scales. If the cat weighs 4 kilograms, which two sacks of sand do you need to make the scales balance as they do in the picture?

1 kg   2 kg   3 kg

Whizzo the wizard and his young assistant Zoog have made a rabbit appear. Who do you think is heavier, Whizzo or Zoog? Who is heavier than the rabbit?

In the vaults of the Loot Bank, Fat Sam and Thin Tim are filling their sacks with money and gold.

Fat Sam's sack is full of bank notes and Thin Tim's sack is full of gold which is much heavier.

Both the sacks are the same size but only Fat Sam gets away. Why does Fat Sam manage to escape?

Clever Clogs has 4 tricky questions for you to answer.

100gm

100gm

Is 100 grams of lead heavier than 100 grams of feathers? Why are there so many feathers?

Which is heavier, the pile of cushions or the pile of bricks? Which pile is bigger?

Shapes and solids

A square has 4 straight edges of equal length set at right angles to each other.

A cube has 6 square faces, 8 corners and 12 edges.

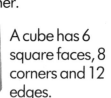

Here is an oblong. How many edges has it? How is it different from a square?

How many edges has a circle?

A cylinder has 2 flat faces and 1 curved face. Can it roll?

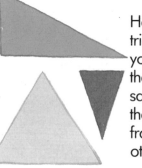

Here are some triangles. Can you spot how they are the same? How are they different from each other?

Baby Brains

Baby Brains is playing with a cardboard cube. She is trying to work out how it is made.

She 'peels' the cube and when she has finished it looks like this.

It is called the 'net' of a cube. You can find nets of other solids.

Rolling shapes

A ball shape is called a sphere. It rolls because it has a curved face. How many spheres can you see in this picture?

What shape is the soldier boy's drum? Is there anything else in the picture which is the same shape?

Shape patterns

The orange shape is a hexagon. How many edges has it? A honeycomb is made of hexagons fitted together. When shapes

fit together without gaps, it is called a tessellation. Do circles tessellate? Can you see a tessellation of hexagons?

In a cottage kitchen

Look carefully at this picture

How many different shapes can you find?
Can you name them all?
How many tessellations can you see?
Look again at the opposite page. Have you
found all the shapes on that page?

Look around at home and see how many
shapes and solids you can find.
The kitchen is a good place to look.
Find out if the solids you find roll or whether
you can build with them.
Try drawing any shapes you find and see if
you can make tessellations from them.

Multiplying

Digby Hall has 4 rows of windows and 3 windows in each row. This makes 12 windows altogether. In maths code you would write 4 × 3 = 12.

Coloured Squares

Count these squares. What do you find out?

2 × 6

4 × 3

1 × 12

6 × 2

3 × 4

12 × 1

How Many Altogether?

How many stamps? 6 × 8 = ?

How many eggs? 2 × 3 = ?

How many squares of chocolate? 4 × 5 = ?

How many sheeps' legs? 4 × 4 = ?

How many fingers? 5 × 4 = ?

Multiplication Wheel

This flower has 5 petals

How many petals do 6 flowers have?

1 × 5 = 5
2 × 5 = 10
3 × 5 = 15
4 × 5 = 20
5 × 5 = 25
6 × 5 = 30
7 × 5 = 35
8 × 5 = 40
9 × 5 = 45
10 × 5 = 50

Polly has 9 bits of clothing. How many two-piece outfits can she make from them?

Count the tops, then the bottoms, then the different outfits.

If Polly only wanted to make 3 two-piece outfits, how many bits of clothing would she need?

How many fleas?

There once was a woman who had 7 husbands. Each husband had 7 cats.

Each cat had 7 kittens.

Each kitten had 7 fleas.

How many fleas were there altogether?

Dividing

If you wanted to share 12 chicks equally among 4 children, how many would you give to each?

12 divided by 4 equals 3.
$(12 \div 4 = 3)$

If one palm tree can only hold 4 monkeys ...

How many trees would 12 monkeys need?

Ready Reckoner

You can use this ready reckoner to work out multiplication and division sums. It is very easy to use.

$12 \div 3$

To find 12 divided by 3, run your finger along the 3 row until you reach 12, or find the square marked 12 and read the column and row that link at the square. This shows you that:

$12 \div 3 = 4$ or $12 \div 4 = 3$
$3 \times 4 = 12$ $4 \times 3 = 12$

Using the ready reckoner, can you find the answers to these sums?
$6 \div 2$; $6 \div 3$; 3×3; 2×3; 5×4; 4×5; $20 \div 4$; $20 \div 5$.

28

1	2	3	4	5	6	7
2	4	6	8	10	12	14
3	6	9	12	15	18	21
4	8	12	16	20	24	28
5	10	15	20	25	30	35
6	12	18	24	30	36	42
7	14	21	28	35	42	49

These 33 lollipops have to be shared equally among 11 children. How many can they each have?

Trick Question

How many times can you take this number ... from this one?

Equal shares

Will there be equal shares for everyone? Will there be anything left over?

Odd numbers and even numbers

Numbers that can be divided by 2 are called even numbers. All the rest are called odd numbers. Are the gorillas wearing even or odd numbers? What about the geese?

Fractions

If something is divided into two equal parts we call each part a half. In maths code we write this as ½.

2 half pieces  put back together again look like one whole orange.

Our maths code says ½ + ½ = 2/2 = 1.

In a fraction the number beneath the line tells you how many pieces of equal size make up the whole.

The number above the line tells you how many pieces are being used. The fraction ½ means 1 out of 2 pieces of equal size.

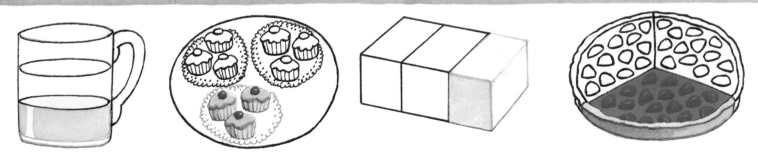

When something is divided into 3 equal parts we call each part one third – ⅓.

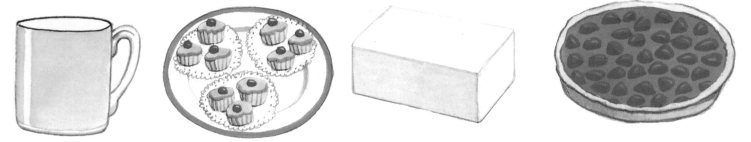

If you put the three equally sized parts back together again, you have the whole.

Who will have the bigger slice of cake?

I WANT ⅛ OF THE CAKE

I WANT ⅐

2 out of 8 frogs are doing handstands. 2/8 of the frogs are doing handstands.

What fraction of the penguins are carrying umbrellas?

The Art Class

How many children are there in the class? What fraction of them have fair hair? What fraction of them are wearing striped shirts?

What fraction of them are painting?
What fraction of them are modelling clay?
What fraction of them are being naughty?

Farmer Brown's Cows

Farmer Brown had a fine herd of black and white cows.

He took half of them to a market and sold them.

He gave ¼ of the herd to a lady who had a dairy.

⅛ of the herd escaped from their field one stormy night.

The only cows Farmer Brown had left were Daisy, Dewdrop and Doris. How many cows did he have in the herd to start with?

Night and Day

LICE

What do you see at night?

What do you see in the daytime?

See how Clever Clogs spends the 24 hours of the day.

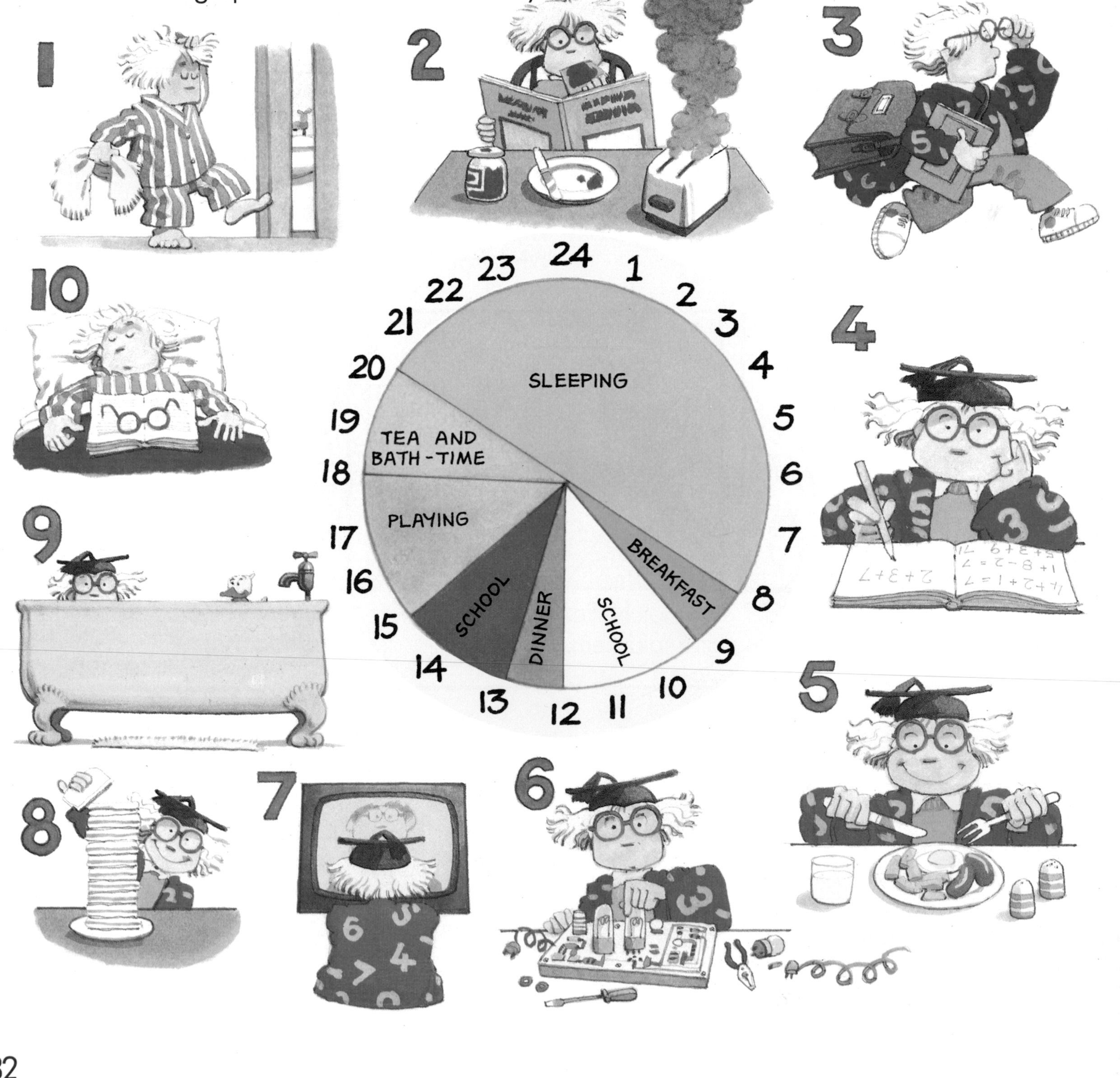
1
2
3
4
5
6
7
8
9
10
24 1 2 3 4 5 6 7 8 9 10 11 12 13 14 15 16 17 18 19 20 21 22 23
SLEEPING
BREAKFAST
SCHOOL
DINNER
SCHOOL
PLAYING
TEA AND
BATH-TIME

The Seasons

Spring

March   April   May

Summer

June   July   August

Autumn

September   October   November

In which season is Christmas? In which season is your birthday? Which seasons do you think belong with these things: frost, harvest, buds, icicles, picnics, skiing, going to the seaside,

Winter

December   January   February

ice skating, halloween, strawberries, baked potatoes, apples, ice cream, barbecues, lambs, robins, blossom, tadpoles, conkers, holly berries, acorns?

Calendar Questions

Look at this calendar.
How many days are schooldays this month? If Sam goes to football every Saturday, how many times will he go to football this month?

Look at a calendar to help you answer the next questions.

How many months are there in a year?
How many months have 30 days?
How many months have 31 days?
Which is the shortest month of the year?
What is the name of the ninth month?
In which month is your birthday?
In which month is Easter this year?
In which month is St. Valentine's Day?
What is a Leap Year?

MAY						
SUN	MON	TUES	WED	THURS	FRI	SAT
					1	2
3	4	5	6	7	8	9
10	11	12	13	14	15	16
17	18	19	20	21	22	23
24	25	26	27	28	29	30
31						

Measuring time

The sun has always governed our measure of time. The Egyptians used shadow clocks like this. It pointed towards the sun and the shadow of the crossbar fell on an hour scale.

Later on people invented sundials like this to measure time. The shadow of the dial fell on a marked circle rather like a clock face. You can still see sundials today in some places.

The Egyptians also used water clocks – bowls with marks on the inside which could be read as the water dripped out.

King Alfred used a candle clock which took four hours to burn away. He kept it in a place where there were no draughts.

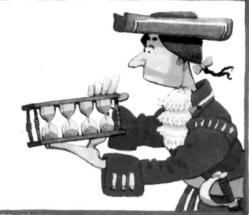

Seamen used to measure time with sand clocks. They used them to help work out the speed the ship was moving.

Simple Clocks

You can make simple clocks of your own. Here are some easy ones to try. What other types of clock could you make?

Candle Clock

Stick pins into a candle at regular intervals, then stand it firmly on a tin lid and light it. As the candle burns, the pins will drop on to the tin lid. The time it takes the candle to burn from one pin to the next can be called a pin unit.

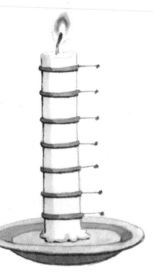

Sand Clock

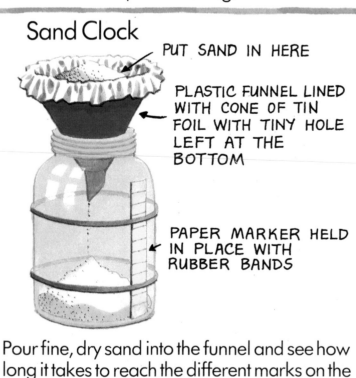

PUT SAND IN HERE

PLASTIC FUNNEL LINED WITH CONE OF TIN FOIL WITH TINY HOLE LEFT AT THE BOTTOM

PAPER MARKER HELD IN PLACE WITH RUBBER BANDS

Pour fine, dry sand into the funnel and see how long it takes to reach the different marks on the paper scale.

How long do you think it takes you to do the things in the pictures?
Do you think they take more or less time to do than it says?

What can you do in ONE SECOND?

clap your hands?

read a whole book?

blink?

What can you do in TEN SECONDS?

drink a glass of milk?

do a jigsaw puzzle?

eat a plate of spaghetti?

What can you do in FIVE MINUTES?

make a cake?

get dressed?

cycle 20 kilometres?

What can you do in ONE HOUR?

paint a picture?

paint a house?

mow the lawn?

What is the time on each of these clocks?

The cuckoo only comes out on the hour. How long will it be until he next comes out?

What times do these watches and clock show? One of them shows a different time from the others. Which of them is the odd one out?

The story of counting

Thousands of years ago, people did not know how to count so they used sign language instead.

The first people to count used their fingers to count up to ten. These shepherds need to count to more than ten, so the first is counting ones, the second tens and the third counts hundreds.

The shepherds knew how many sheep they had but they needed a way to remember the number.

So they made three piles of pebbles, one for units, one for tens and one for hundreds.

Some people, like the Mayas, used their fingers and toes to count in twenties.

The ancient Egyptians cut small notches on a wooden tally stick so that they could remember the numbers they counted.

The Egyptians invented the first calculator. They made grooves in the sand and moved pebbles along them just like an abacus.

They were also the first to give numbers symbols so they could write them down. They used a tool to make marks on a clay tablet.

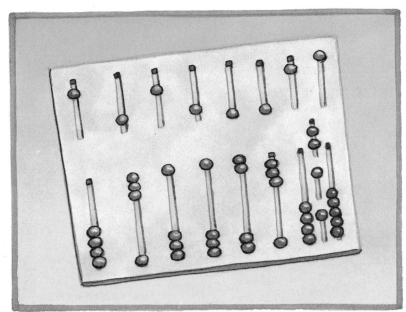

The Ancient Romans used this small metal abacus. They could do simple adding and taking away sums by moving the pebbles along the slots.

At school, Roman children learnt these numbers. They wrote the numbers on wax tablets with a pointed stick. Can you read the numbers?

Roman numbers were used for a long time, but it was very difficult to do sums with them.

This is because there was no zero or place value. The Hindus had a much better number system, but

no one outside India knew about it. Then an Arab scribe went to India and decided to copy it.

He showed it to people in Italy and they copied it too. Can you recognise the 2, 3 and 0 from the numbers the scribe has drawn?

The Hindu numbers could be used for the most complicated sums. By the sixteenth century everyone in Europe used them.

Today we still use the Hindu number system although the shape of the numbers and the way we use them has changed quite a bit.

A world without numbers

Can you imagine what the world would be like without numbers? In these pictures all the numbers are missing. See how many missing numbers you can find.

Counting machines

For thousands of years people have thought up ways of working out long, difficult sums quickly.

The simple machines they invented were early types of calculators.

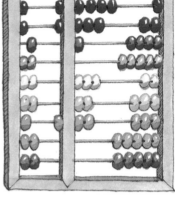

THE BEADS ON THIS SIDE OF THE CENTRAL BAR EACH HAVE A VALUE OF 5

THESE BEADS EACH HAVE A VALUE OF ONE

THE BEADS ARE MOVED TOWARDS THE CENTRAL BAR TO RECORD THE NUMBERS

Counting frames like this abacus were first used 3000 years ago and still are today.
Some Japanese work out sums on them so fast that you can hardly see their fingers move.

A few hundred years ago people began to use mathematical tables – lists of numbers which you look up to work out sums quickly.

Later on slide rules were invented. You can do difficult sums with these by sliding one numbered part of the rule against the other.

Brunsviga calculator

counting machine

pocket calculator

The first calculating machines were mechanical adding machines. You had to set some levers, then crank a handle to work the machine. Next

there were electrical counting machines. Modern calculators use integrated circuits. They work quickly and accurately, yet are small and cheap.

Computers

A computer is an electronic machine. It can store information and do sums but it cannot think by itself. It has to be given information and told what to do with it. This is called programming. Computers can carry out thousands of instructions in a second.

Early computers were big and expensive and did not always work very well. They could do little more than a modern calculator.

The invention of the microchip made it possible to make computers smaller and cheaper. One day you might have your own pocket computer.

Using a Computer

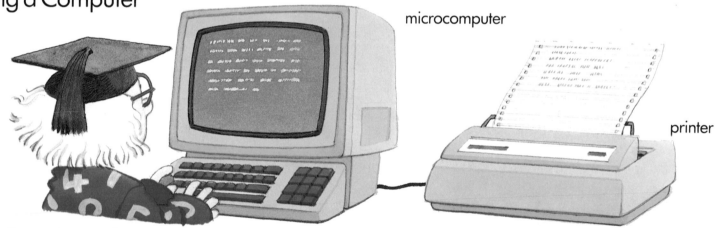

microcomputer

printer

The information or data you give to a computer is called the input. To feed the data into the computer, you type it on to a keyboard.

The results which come out of the computer are called the output and can be shown on a screen. They can also be printed on paper by a printer.

```
10 PRINT "ROBOT INVADERS"
20 LET H=0
30 FOR T=1 TO 25
40 FOR I=1 TO INT(RND*30+20)
50 NEXT I
60 LET A=INT(RND*20)
70 LET D=INT(RND*15)
80 LET P$=CHR$(INT(RND*53+11))
90 CLS
100 FOR J=0 TO D
110 PRINT
120 NEXT J
130 PRINT TAB(A);P$.
140 FOR I=1 TO 15
```

Computers can be programmed through the keyboard. Here is part of a program written in BASIC★, one of the many computer languages.

*Beginners All Purpose Symbolic Instruction Code

The computer has a memory which stores data. Extra data can be stored in number form on tapes or discs which can be used when needed.

Amazing number facts

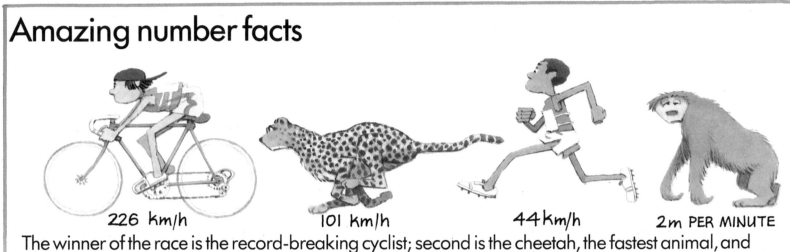

226 km/h 101 km/h 44 km/h 2m PER MINUTE

The winner of the race is the record-breaking cyclist; second is the cheetah, the fastest animal, and the fastest man came third. The sloth, the slowest animal, would really be out of the picture. Where do you think 1) you would be and 2) a snail would come in the race?

The largest . . .

The world's largest toyshop is Hamley's in London. The shop covers 4,180 square metres.

The largest living bird is the North African ostrich. This one is 2.74 m tall.

The largest Easter egg ever made was 5m high. How high do you think the largest goose egg is?

The heaviest carnivore was a Kodiak bear. It weighed 757 kg.

The heaviest lettuce grown in Britain weighed over 11kg.

In 1984, the heaviest dog was a St Bernard who weighed 140kg.

The longest...

One of the longest sausages ever made was 3km long. It was cooked and eaten by boy scouts at the Great Children's Party in Hyde Park in London on 30th May 1979.

The smallest...

The Stegosaurus, which weighed 1¾ tonnes, had the smallest brain compared to the size of its body. The brain weighed 70g.

The smallest British mammal is the Pygmy Shrew. This is its real size and it weighs about 4g.

Amazing feats

The most hamburgers ever eaten by 1 person is 21 in 9 minutes.

The youngest person to write a book was 4 years old.

Mr Shri N. Ravi from India balanced on one leg for 34 hours.

Records

The world's top-selling drink is Coca Cola. 301m bottles are sold a day in 155 countries.

The fastest time for a round-the-world flight is 45 hrs. The distance covered was 39,147 km.

The highest number with a name is a centrillion. It is 10^{600} or 1 with 600 noughts after it.

Number puzzles

The children holding the balloons are standing in sequence. Can you see what the sequence is?

How many balloons should the baby in blue be holding to continue the sequence?

Triangular Numbers

1   **3**   **6**   **10**

How many acrobats would there be in a fifth group in this sequence? Look carefully at the difference in numbers in each of the groups. Does this pattern fit? +1, +2, +3 continuing.

Square Numbers

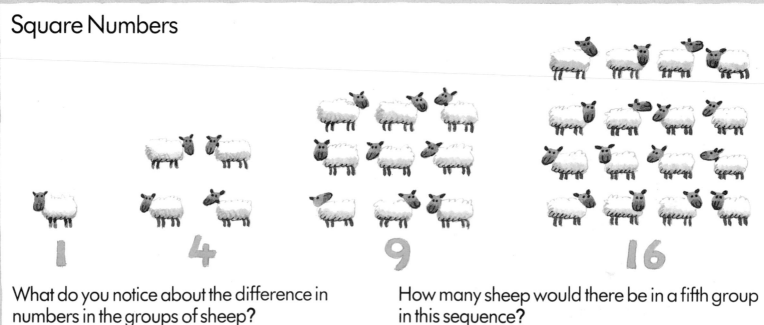

1   **4**   **9**   **16**

What do you notice about the difference in numbers in the groups of sheep?

How many sheep would there be in a fifth group in this sequence?

Magic Squares

In the first of these squares the numbers must add up to 34 in every direction. In the second square they must add up to 65. Can you work out where the missing numbers should go?

Special Numbers

Some numbers are special and you can do things with them that you cannot do with other numbers. The number 9 has special qualities. Look at this:

$$1 \times 9, + 2 = 11$$
$$12 \times 9, + 3 = 111$$
$$123 \times 9, + 4 = 1111$$
$$1234 \times 9, + 5 = 11111$$
$$12345 \times 9, + 6 = 111111$$
$$123456 \times 9, + 7 = 1111111$$
$$1234567 \times 9, + 8 = 11111111$$
$$12345678 \times 9, + 9 = 111111111$$

Another Number Nine Trick

Add the digits of any number and subtract them from the original number. The number will always be 9, or be divisible by 9. For example:

Take a number			783
Add the digits	$7 + 8 + 3$	=	18
Subtract the second number from the first one	$783 - 18$	=	765

$$765 \div 9 = 85$$

Try the trick with more numbers.

Perfect Numbers

A perfect number is one that is the sum of all its factors (its divisors). 6 is a perfect number. Its factors are 3, 2 and 1 and they add up to 6. There is a perfect number between 25 and 30. Can you work out what it is?

Backwards and Forwards Numbers

Some numbers are palindromic. This means that they are the same whichever end you read them from. Look at what happens when you multiply the following numbers.

$$11 \times 11 = 121$$
$$111 \times 111 = 12321$$
$$1111 \times 1111 = 1234321$$
$$11111 \times 11111 = 123454321$$
$$111111 \times 111111 = 12345654321$$

Quick Number Puzzle

Think of a number less than 5
Add 5
Double this
Subtract 10
Divide by 2

What do you notice about the answer? Try the trick with the other numbers under 5. What do you notice about all the answers?

Glossary

These are the symbols used in this book:

>	is greater than
<	is less than
=	is the same as or equals
+	add or put together
—	take away or subtract
×	multiply
÷	divide or share
8	eight or eight objects

All numbers are symbols of quantity. You cannot pick up two but you can pick up two sweets.

add	Put two or more sets of things together (p. 16).
angle	Region between two meeting lines or surfaces (p.24).
balance	Have equal weight on each side (p.22).
birthday	The date you were born. Your birthday party is not always on your birthday.
boundary	A containing line closed around some things (p.8).
code	A set of words or symbols standing in place of something else (p.9). SEE Signs as Symbols.
column	Things or figures arranged one above the other (p. 10).
divide	Separate into equal portions (p.28).
edge	The meeting line of two surfaces of a solid (p.24).
equals	Has the same number as.
even number	A number which will divide by two leaving no remainder (p.29).
face	One of the surfaces making up a shape (p.24).
fraction	Always refers back to something which has been cut or divided into equal parts (p.30).
mathematics	The study of number and space.
member	One of the things in a set (p.8).
multiply	Add together many sets of the same number (p.26).
net	The opening out of a solid so that all the faces can be seen. Lines show you where to fold it to make it back into a solid (p.24).
numbers	Names given to counting symbols
odd numbers	Numbers which have remainder when divided by two (p.29).
partition	Draw a line through a set to separate it into more parts (p.8).
set	A number of things having something in common (p.8).
sequence	Things that belong next to each other on some principle of order
share	Divide equally.
solid	A shape which has three dimensions (p.24).
sub-set	Part of a set with a property common to its members different from the one common to the whole set (p.8).
sum	Total, the result of adding.
take away	Make less by removing a sub-set from a set of things (p. 18).
tessellation	Shapes fitting together and leaving no gaps (p.24).